Two Beautiful Women for Him

Hot Erotic Short Stories Illustrated with

Hentai Pictures

_____

Emily White

Printing and distribution: Heinz-Beusen-Stieg 5 22926 Ahrensburg, Germany

TABLE OF CONTENTS

INTRODUCTION

Welcome to a captivating journey where my enthralling stories seamlessly intertwine with enchanting illustrations that redefine the very essence of desire in the world of hentai erotica.

Within the secret pages of these forbidden tales, I invite you to immerse yourself in a fiery universe of unrestrained passion. Every word is a whispered moan, and each illustration is a visual embrace that transforms the realms of fantasy into tangible reality.

This collection is not for the faint of heart. It's a bold manifesto, an invitation urging you to delve into the dark depths of lust, where pleasure is painted with audacious strokes and details that promise to quicken the rhythm of your heart. The illustrations are provocative gateways, guiding you into sensual dimensions where every hidden desire finds its expression without remorse.

Are you ready to plunge into a whirlwind of seduction and temptation, where the pages themselves transform into a stage for your most secret fantasies? Allow yourself to be carried away into a realm where sin transforms into art, and art seamlessly merges harmoniously with the ecstasy of desire.

Lift the cover and prepare for an experience ignited by the flame of passion. This is not just another collection; it's your exclusive ticket to the boldest manifestations of anime eros, written masterfully by me, **Emily White**.

BEAUTIFUL MOTHER IN LAW

My name is Eusebio, 28 years old, married to Monique, 26 years old, beautiful , charming, brown hair with blue eyes.

We live in the outskirts of a medium-sized provincial town, in a small villa.

It's July, it's hot, the vacations are in two weeks, we can't think of anything else. That morning I am on vacation, working at home when the phone rings. My wife Monique tells me that her mother has just been admitted to the emergency room of the hospital G...., she sprained her ankle.

Monique can't leave the store and asks me to go see what exactly is going on. I put on a clean shirt, change out of my Bermuda shorts and off I go. The hospital is a 20-minute drive away. When I arrive, I immediately see my mother-in-law, Luce (58, brunette, well preserved from three weekly gym sessions) in the emergency room waiting room.

Her treatment is over, she only has an ankle to knee cast on her right leg.

Me: - Hi Luce, what do you say?

Mom: - Oh dear, I slipped on the stairs and sprained my ankle. Can you take me home?

Me: - Sure, I'll bring the car right away.

Once parked just outside the ward, to help her because she obviously doesn't know how to walk with crutches, I tell her to put her arm around my neck and use the crutch on my other arm. This way she keeps her balance.

She is dressed in a light navy blue dress with a U-shaped neckline and a zipper down her back that reaches above her knees. I grab her by the waist and we walk to the car. During this short walk, she is pressed against me, and putting her arm around my neck distorts her cleavage, giving me a deep view inside. She's wearing a black balconette bra, the upper curve of her big white tits standing out. She hops a little on her good foot, which allows me to see her nipples in the underwire.

When we get to the car, I open the front passenger door and move the seat all the way back, so she is comfortable. She sits down with the help of her good leg, the left, while the other one stays out of the car on the ground. As I help her sit down, I look at her cleavage and the nice cleavage between her big tits, at one point I almost put my nose in it. Now I help her pull her right leg in, plastered, I squat down; the fact that I have one leg in and one leg out at this moment, forces her to spread her thighs, her dress is pulled up when she sits, I almost have my head in the way, I have a terrible erection, I see her black panties, the hair coming out of them, she has a tuft like my wife, very thick and dense, she makes a bulge at the level of her pubic bone in her panties.

I gently pull at her injured leg, and as I stand up my hand rests on her thigh just above the knee. She pretends not to notice. I take my place behind the wheel and we drive to her house, a thirty-minute drive away in a nearby village.

She falls asleep on the way, perhaps given painkillers. As she falls asleep, Mom has completely relaxed, the tops of her boobs rising and falling in her cleavage to the rhythm of her breathing. Her dress is pulled up almost to the top of her thighs, from my driver's seat I can see her panties and I realize that Monique, my wife, has inherited her mother's thick hair pussy.

At this moment I have a terrible erection, I'm too tight in my Bermuda shorts, so much the worse, I pull down the elastic as well as that of my underwear below my balls, I have to pull out my cock, I feel like masturbating, my mother-in-law turns me on. At a country crossroads, in the middle of sunflower fields, I decide to leave the road and take a farm road. After about fifty meters I park in a place where there are some trees, we are no longer visible from the road. I put my right arm around her neck and move my hand along her cleavage.

I lightly caress the top of her boobs, then spread the bottom with the back of my hand and feel her boobs. They must have given her a dose of horse painkillers in the emergency room because she's not moving. With my free hand I grab her left hand and lock my cock in, too bad she can't jerk me off.

She really seems completely out of it, now I sink both hands into her panties and pull out her big tits. She has slightly bigger tits than her daughter, I massage them, knead them, play with her tits, they get hard even while she's sleeping, I can't take it anymore, I start sucking and sucking them.

While I suck her tits, I put my left hand on the inside of her left thigh, I go up to her panties. With my index finger I massage her slit up and down through the fabric, my finger gets wet, she gets wet in her sleep the slut. I pull the fabric and insert a finger into her slit, she is warm and wet. Suddenly I hear the sound of an engine, definitely a tractor, I stick my cock in my bermuda shorts, I put my mother-in-law's tits back in her panties.

A farmer passes by with his car on the road, looks at the car, then continues on his way, he must be used to it. Also, upon closer inspection, I notice that there are several Kleenex scattered on the ground in our makeshift parking lot. This is the moment my mother-in-law chooses to wake up.

Mother-in-law: - But .... where are we? I think I fell asleep.

Me: - Yes, I had to stop, um, natural need.

Mother-in-law: - Oh, right, yeah, I should do that too.... I feel like I'm fine, it's weird, must be the sedatives from the hospital.

Me: - You're probably right, Luce.

Phew! She doesn't seem to notice anything, but I would have liked to continue.

Me: - Can't you wait until you get home for your needs?

Mother-in-law: - No, it's urgent right now.

Me: - I will help you out. But it won't be easy for you, for ...

Mother-in-law - I use the door and get up.

So, he gets out, first his injured leg, another seen in his groin, then the other. She leans with her left arm on the open door and with the other on a crutch.

Mother-in-law: - Um... you're going to have to help me, Eusebio.

Me: - Do you really want me to do that?

Mother-in-law: - We can't do otherwise.

I squat down in front of her, put my hands under her dress, take her panties from the elastic on her hips and pull them down to her feet, remove them completely.

I still have an erection breaking through the shorts. She lets go of the crutch and presses it against the doorframe, with her free hand she lifts her dress up in front, moves her pelvis forward a bit and arches her back, she begins to pee shamelessly in front of me.

At first it flows like a waterfall and then in a fine net, almost like a man. She watches herself piss, I don't lose sight of her for a moment, the spray comes out of her bush in a curve, you can barely make out her pink slit, the hair is so thick.

I pull down my shorts and panties and jerk off as I smell her panties.

Mother-in-law: - It feels good to let it all go when you want it so badly. Do you like it?

Me: - You are really turning me on, Luce.

Mother-in-law: - Can I have it back?

Me: - Huh? What?

Mother-in-law: - Well, my panties, can I have them back?

Me: - Yes, wait!

I stand in front of her, who still has her dress on, and run my panties over her slit, wipe off the remaining piss, run it over my face and lick it off. The taste of the piss is quite sour.

Me: - What a clump Luce! You know, Monique inherited a nice one too.

I know, we talk about it sometimes. Come on, enough playing, let's go home.

Me: - Oh no Luce, you can't leave me like this, look at the erection I have.

Mother-in-law: - Come on, you've had enough haven't you? I'll leave you my panties if you want.

Me: - OK, let's go home. Do you want me to help you?

Mother-in-law: - No, I'll try to get by.

Using the door jambs, she takes a seat and, taking the knee of her cast leg with both hands, lifts her leg and sits down. I stay facing her in case she needs help, which gives me another good view of her beard as she spreads her legs. I leave her panties twisted around my cock, pull up my shorts, and get back behind the wheel. For the rest of the drive he dozes off.

We get to her house, start again as before, I help her out of the car and we go into the living room, I sit her down on the couch.

Me: - I get the crutches from the car.

Mother-in-law: - You are very kind, Eusebio, thank you.

A moment later I come back, my mother-in-law has stood up, she must have lost her balance a bit, and is leaning with both arms outstretched on the coffee table in the living room.

Mother-in-law: - I tried to get up to see if I could make it on my own but it's not possible.

I'm facing her; in this position, leaning forward on the coffee table, I can't take my eyes off the two white masses of her boobs in her cleavage.

Me: - I will help you.

I leave her in her position (almost doggy style), I take a stool on which I support her leg in plaster, the other one remains on the floor.

Mother-in-law: - But ..... do you leave me like this?

Me: - Your leg is elevated, isn't it?

Mom: - Help me sit on a chair, please.

Me: - Not yet.

I move the chairs and couch away from the coffee table so she has no other possible support. I stand behind her, kneel on the carpet and tuck my head under her dress. I pull my cock out of my shorts and begin to masturbate, still with her panties on.

Mother-in-law: - Finally, Eusebio! What ...? Have you gone crazy?

I let go of my cock and stroke his thighs, run a hand through his front bush and then touch his buttocks with both hands.

Me: - What a handsome bearded man, what an ass, I love looking under your skirts Luce.

Mother-in-law: - Stop it!

Me: - You turned me on earlier, look at my erection!

I get up, dropping her panties on the floor, lift her dress up over her rump, look at her with her ass on the table, a little panicked. I walk up to her, a little to the side because of the table, looking into her eyes, sinking a hand into her cleavage.

Me: - Ohh what beautiful tits, I want to see them.

I unzip her dress, take it off and unhook her bra. Her two big tits hang below her like nipples. I feel them, massage them, squat down to suck them, the nipples are hard, I take the opportunity to also stick a finger in her pussy, she is wet.

Mother-in-law: - Come on Eusèbe, be reasonable!

Me: - I've been fantasizing about you for ages, mother-in-law.

Mother-in-law: - But you are not going to ....

Me: - You peed in front of me just now, you are not a saint? And you're wet, so that turns you on!

I get completely naked. I position myself in front of her face, straddling the table and holding my cock in one hand, I grab her by the hair with the other, I don't need to talk, she opens her mouth and I push my cock in.

Me: - There you go mom, that's right, suck me. Stroke your tits, be a bitch!

I give her slow pelvic motions, I fuck her mouth which she has opened wide, she inhales well, it slides down her throat.

Me: - Now jerk off.

She looks at me and puts a finger in her pussy, on which she makes small back movements.

Me: - You're good Luce, yes, keep going, I'm going to squirt.

At these words she moans and accelerates the masturbation of her pussy and I accompany her by accelerating the pace, I am about to cum and so is she. Suddenly there is an explosion, I squirt, she screams and comes too.

Me: - Ahhhhhhhhhhh here! here! bitch! I'm unloading all over you!

I send four spurts of cum at her and hold her head so she swallows it all. She can't contain it, the juice flows from the corners of her lips onto her chin and falls onto the coffee table.

Mother-in-law: - Oh dear, Eusebio, you can imagine, I came. Did you enjoy it?

Me: - It was really good, Luce.

Mother-in-law: - Kiss me!

I put my lips on hers and we roll around, full of my juices. She puts her tongue inside me and I suck it out. I have just been pumped by my mother-in-law, unbelievable! I'm so horny I can barely move. Now I get behind my mother-in-law and point my cock at her slit, I take her doggy style; she's wet, with one thrust of my kidney I'm in.

Me: - Here, take it deep in your pussy, I will fuck you.

Mother-in-law: - Ahhh yes Eusebio, take me, I want you.

I grab onto her hips and fill her with my loins. I bend over her back to massage her big tits. She allows herself well, moves her buttocks on my cock, feels pleasure and moans.

Me: - Do you feel good now, dirty girl?

Mother-in-law: - Yes, honey, go ahead and do it again, it feels good.

Me: - Tell me you're my dirty girl!

Mother-in-law: - Yes, Eusebio, I'm your pig.

Me: - Stick a finger in your ass, keep being a slut!

While I'm still sticking her doggy style, she puts her middle finger in her ass and pushes it in and out.

Me:- But you do everything I say, you're a real bitch!

Mother-in-law:- Ahhh, I'm your bitch, yes, keep going, keep going!

Her anus expands a bit with her finger filing it, the excitement raise up.

Me: - I'm going to fuck you, slut! Tell me you want me to fuck you.

Mother-in-law: - Yes, go ahead and fuck me, I want to feel your cock in my ass.

Me: - Your daughter loves it! You know how she likes to have her ass photographed?

Mother-in-law: - Yes, I know, we both like it.

I pull my cock out of her pussy and present my glans on her round one. I'm about to sodomize my wife's mother, this is crazy! I spread a buttock with my thumb and begin to thrust. The glans enters slowly and disappears into the anal canal, I keep pushing, it's a little tight, pull the brake but eventually I manage to get it all in until my balls stop.

Mother-in-law: - It hurts, but it feels good.

Me: - You have my cock up your slutty ass, I'm about to fill your ass.

I begin to fill her anus, once again holding her by the hips. Her dilated washer expands to glans size as it almost reaches the edge and then retracts on the shaft as I push into her bowels. I started to file slowly but now the pleasure is mounting and I speed up and give her big thrusts, like I'm in her pussy, I'm pounding my mother-in-law's ass. She is screaming louder and louder from pain and pleasure, she is groping her tits, she is also putting a finger in her pussy, she is titillating her clit, she has completely forgotten about the cast, she is about to cum again, just like me.

Sometimes I pull my cock out completely, pass it up and down her slit, and push it back into her ass, which has expanded to the size of my cock. We reach orgasm at the same time. She takes her foot, continuing to scream loudly, and I push it all the way out into her ass.

Me: - Yes, bitch, I'm cumming in your ass! Hold my cum! Hold it! Hold it!

Mother-in-law: - Ahhhhhhhhhhhhh I'm enjoying it!

We stay frozen for a moment, just long enough for me to relax a bit, I pull my cock out of her ass and cum drips from her dilated anus onto her thighs, onto the stool.

Tuuuuuut! Tuuuuuuut!

Me: - Shit! Monique.... we didn't see the time pass!

I completely unzip immediately, put the chairs back as best I can, move the footrest and put Luce's dress back on and push her onto the couch, put her panties and bra in the pocket of my shorts. It was an emergency!

It's my wife Monique who has just arrived, visiting her mother who has been in a cast and is basically 'sick'. My dick hurts, the brake must have chafed during the fuck.

***

Monique: - Hi! How are you, mom?

Mother-in-law: - Hum! Well, thanks, you see, I have to stay in a cast for a while and I have painkillers.

Monique: - How about you, dear?

Me: - I'm fine, now your mother will rest at home, quietly. Have you told your father?

Monique: - Yes, of course, but he won't be here until 8pm.

But ...... It smells funny in here, doesn't it?

It must smell like cum and wet, but Mom and I don't realize it because we were "in". Even the panties in my pocket are making a wet spot there, they must smell like love too.

Me: - Do you think so? No? Well, I'm going to go get some drinks.

I'm going to the kitchen to get some sodas. I serve them on the coffee table, crap! I discreetly put the tray on top. Monique sits next to her mother on the couch and I sit across from her in an armchair. The two women pay no attention to the position of their legs, so I admire my mother's topknot and my wife's white panties, which nonchalantly keep her thighs apart, her skirt already not the longest.

Monique: - Did you move the chairs? They are not .....

Me: - Hm! I moved the chairs a little to make room for your mother, she can't move easily, they were too close together.

Monique: - Look, what's that in your pocket? It's wet.

Me: - Oh it's nothing, I must have stained myself in the kitchen.

I get up and go back to the kitchen, put some water on the cum that is soaking my bermudas, throw my panties and underwear in the cleaning supplies under the sink. I come back with two cokes, trying to be natural.

Monique: - It smells funny in here, I'm sure of it!

Mother-in-law: - So what do we do? Are you waiting for Rene (my father-in-law) or are you going home?

Me: - I can stay so I don't leave you alone, Luce.

Monique: - Fine, I'll make a small meal and we'll wait for dad, we won't leave mom alone.

Shit. I figured I'd be alone with my mother-in-law for another hour, too bad, after all I got a good lay today, I'll settle for that.

My wife calls me from the kitchen, I join her.

Monique: - Hey, did you notice?

Me: - What?

Monique: - Mom isn't wearing any panties or a bra.

Me: (hypocritically surprised) - The bra, yes.

Monique: - You didn't notice the panties, even though you've been with her since she left the hospital, even in the car, you didn't notice?

Me: - Well, no, although I've helped her in and out of the car and everything... but no.

Monique: - We're going to eat frozen food tonight, not long now.

Me: - OK, I'm going to the living room, you can't leave her alone. She needs to take some medicine, it's 6pm, it's time.

Very naturally, I give the medicine to my beloved mother-in-law and turn on the television. Monique joins me a few minutes later, her mother has fallen asleep. Monique, who has just arrived, lifts her mother's dress and shows me the absence of panties.

Me: - You're right, but what a bearded man, like yours. What a beard, like yours, huh?

Monique: - It's true, I don't have her breasts, but I do have the topknot.

I want to take a shower before dinner, I feel all sweaty and dirty.

Monique: - OK, but how do we do that?

Me: - The easiest way is to take a bath. We put the leg in a plastic bag and keep it out of the bathroom.

- I'll take you to the bathroom, Monique, please get a trash bag.

I renew my support for mom and we stand in front of the bathroom. Monique follows us.

Me: - I will balance you and Monique will take care of your leg.

I get in the bathtub to put my mother-in-law in. Of course, since she's naked under her dress, I've seen her boobs and bush several times, especially when she went over the tub.

Monique: - Well, honey, thank you, I'm going to go help mommy wash up.

Shit. I thought we were going to undress her together. I go back to the kitchen and set the table while I wait, then sit back down in an armchair in the living room. About fifteen minutes later, when I'm asleep, I get a call.

Eusebio! Eusebio!

I go to the bathroom door, which I don't open.

Me: - Yes, what is it?

Monique: - We have a problem, I'm done but I can't lift mom.

Inside I'm thinking I'm lucky today, I'm going to see naked women again.

Me: (hypocritically) - But ..... can I come in?

Mother-in-law: - Come in Eusebio, we're past babyhood, come help us.

Nice view when I enter, the mother-in-law is naked in the bathtub, no foam, her full beard stands out well in the water, and I'm not talking about her big boobs; Monique, leaning forward, her skirt pulled up revealing her white panties, tries to grab her mother by the arm.

Me: - Hold on, honey, you're going to hurt her like that. Leave it to me.

I try to look very 'professional' by giving the impression that I am ignoring my mother-in-law's nudity but my cock betrays me with an erection that distorts my bermuda shorts. I get in the bathtub, stand behind my mother-in-law and weigh her down by putting my arms under her armpits and encircling her tightly.

Me: - Hold your mother as soon as she has her good leg out, you don't want her to slip. She pulls the chair closer, then I get out of the tub and help her sit up.

Once she sits down, Monique goes to get a robe, when she turns back, I'm putting my hands on Mom's boobs and she smiles at me. The fact that I held my mother-in-law naked in my arms makes me hard and it shows.

Mother-in-law: - You are really very helpful Eusèbe, you have a wonderful husband Monique. Oh dear, but you are soaking wet Eusebio, I will lend you a change of clothes.

In fact, while I was helping my mother-in-law, I stuck to her and my clothes got wet. So she is sitting on the chair, in an almost open robe that hides nothing, I am standing to her right, waiting to take her into the living room.

Mother-in-law: - Have you seen Monique, what state is she in?

Monique: - Well yes, it's wet, it's not serious.

Mother-in-law: - But no! Here! (putting her hand on my parts).

Shit! Now my mother-in-law touches me in front of her daughter, as long as she doesn't say anything about what just happened.

Monique: - But that's not fair, mom!

Mother-in-law: - Is it me that has this effect on you, Eusebio?

Me: - It's instinctive, I can't control it .....

Mother-in-law: - Let me see!

She turns to her right, I'm standing at the same level as her face, and pulls down my shorts and pants. My cock jerks, stiff and hard.

Monique: - But mom, you're going crazy! It's your head that should have been treated!

nice - mom: - Let's go! Let's go! Don't make a fuss, he is very devoted, I have to thank him.

I can't think of anything, I don't know what to do or say, my cock is two inches from my stepmother's face.

Mother-in-law: - Give him a gift, honey, he deserves it.

Monique: - But it won't work, poor mom.

My mother-in-law grabs my balls with three fingers (like when you screw in a light bulb) and with her mouth wide open she kisses my glans, then most of my cock, closes her eyes and sucks me. I use light lumbar thrusts to fuck her mouth well. I hold her by pressing her neck to me. My wife remains frozen in place with her mouth open, it's like paralyzed. I don't stay idle, I open my mother-in-law's robe and massage her tits. With her other hand, the stepmother caresses my thighs and buttocks, until I feel a finger in my ass, I feel it going in and out, she is fingering my ass, the whore, it increases my pleasure.

Drink!

Dring!!!!!!!!!

Me: - The phone!

Monique has already gone to answer it, she interrupted me a bit in my pleasure, this unexpected ringing made me jump. My mother-in-law closes her robe, I pull on my Bermuda shorts and take her back into the living room. Monique hangs up.

Mother-in-law: Who was that?

Monique: - Dad, he's broken down on the highway, he'll be back late. That's it, you're done with your dirty work, you know, I could tell him.

Mother-in-law: - Ohh! When you were younger and I would see you putting coke bottles and carrots in your room, secretly, I never said anything.

Monique: - But ......

Mother-in-law: - Do you think I'm stupid, do you think I couldn't hear you shouting, "Yes, yes, etc."? You have a short memory, you didn't come quietly.

Oh, I'm learning a lot about my dear wife, I don't get involved in the conversation, I don't want to take sides. She always comes out loud, that's true.

Mother-in-law: -With all this, Eusebio, we could not finish, go to my room and choose a change of clothes, do not stay like this.

So I go upstairs and pick out a t-shirt and shorts from my father-in-law's wardrobe, I don't take pants or shorts, those are too personal. I take the opportunity to look in my mother-in-law's wardrobe, she has some beautiful sexy lingerie, stockings, garters etc...., I caress for a moment all this beautiful lingerie, unfortunately it only smells of fabric softener. Suddenly I am surprised again, Monique is there in the doorway.

Monique: - And....... Why don't you try it?

Me: - Don't you understand?

Monique: - I would love to see you in there.

Me: - What, you want me to try on lingerie? Ouch - I think your mom isn't the only one who needs her head taken care of.

Monique: - And... If I said.... Things for daddy?

Me: - Shit! Don't fuck it up, honey.

Monique: - Choose, honey, you either make me happy or ....

Me: - Shit! Me: - Shit! I don't! Okay, fine.

I undress and Monique chooses to put on black stockings with a garter belt and a matching bra: she also makes me put on a black thong, I'm in disguise. We go down to the living room, Monique shows me to her mother, spinning me around, making me assume teasing positions, they both laugh at me, I'm a little ashamed to be put on display like this.

Monique: - Have you seen your son-in-law, mom, acting crazy?

Mother-in-law: - He's cute like that. What's in the bra?

I'm standing in front of the couch where my mother-in-law is sitting, Monique next to me lifts the bra on top of my chest and pinches my nipples.

Monique: - She has small breasts, the naughty girl.

Mother-in-law: - Suck on them, honey.

Monique starts to suck on my nipples, which get hard, it even hurts a little because she sucks hard. She pushes me forward to the couch, I am between her mother's thighs and I sit down. Her mother-in-law massages my cock through the fabric of my thong, then spreads it and slowly masturbates me. She has opened her robe, she is naked. Then it's Monique still standing at my side taking my cock in her hand under her mother's eyes. I have another erection.

Monique: - Come on, mom! Suck your son-in-law's cock.

My mother-in-law puts her hands on my buttocks and gives me a blowjob, Monique holds my cock in her hand and jerks me into her mother's mouth; after a moment of pumping she grabs her mother by the hair and slips her mouth into hers, the gaping mouths roll around each other, tongues play around each other, tongues go in and out of her mouth, it's wonderful. Monique caresses her mother's tits, in her excitement she pushes me a little, she kneels between her mother's thighs and sinks her tongue into her pussy, massaging her breasts. Her mother-in-law spreads the lips of her slit so she can lick better, she gets wet profusely. Monique licks the entire slit and insists on the clit which she tickles with her tongue. Unbelievably, my mother-in-law and her daughter get drunk in front of me, I quickly remove my thong and masturbate as I watch. Now Monique slips two fingers into her mother's pussy and with her other hand spreads the skin around her clit to make it protrude and licks it.

Mother-in-law: - Yes, honey, it's good, you're licking well, what a beautiful tongue!

Come over next to me, get fucked my darling, show mommy how you get fucked.

Monique sits next to her mother on the couch, she pulls up her skirt, opens her thighs and spreads her panties, she has the same bush as her mother, I stand in front of her, her mother-in-law takes my cock in her hand and directs it to her daughter's pussy. I penetrate Monique, she enters on her own so wet, I slowly smooth her at first, her mother unbuttoning her blouse, groping her tits while sticking her hands in her panties and rolling her skivvies. I fuck my wife who is having sex with her mother. The mother-in-law leans over Monique's tits and hits her with the application, one after the other, the tits become very hard and erect. The mother-in-law has left her thighs open, I finger her pussy as I fuck Monique lying next to her. She is moaning, she is wet, the pleasure is mounting.

Mother-in-law: - Fuck her Eusèbe, she will lick me.

Me: - Right away Luce, you heard Monique, get in position Monique, I'm about to fuck your ass.

My wife doggy style on the floor, rests her forearms on her mother's thighs, sitting on the couch, and begins to lick her slit. I pull her skirt up over her loins, pull her panties down over her thighs, run my tongue over her slit, wet the grommet and insert my glans. I push slowly, my wife's ass widens to let my glans pass, I stop, then in one stroke I push my whole cock into Monique's circle.

Monique: - Aaiiieeee! Bastard, you're tearing me apart.

Mother-in-law: - Lick my baby, lick mommy, make me come.

Me: - Ohhhhhh Luce, I'm filling your darling daughter's ass.

Mother-in-law: - Jerk yourself off too honey, we're about to cum together.

Me: - Look at your daughter, half dressed, tits out, skirt up, panties down, getting fucked, a real slut.

My mother-in-law is having her clit licked, moving her pelvis up and down on her daughter's expert tongue, Monique is fingering herself while I take her ass and hold her by the hips, all three of us reach orgasm.

Mother-in-law: - Yes, I'm coming, I'm coming!!!!!!!!

Monique: - Ahhhhhh yes, my ass!!!!! It's good.

Me: - Ahhhhhhhhh, I'm cumming, I'm cumming, here! Here! in your ass! ahhhhhh

I release four squirts into my wife's anus, when I pull out my cock, it's dripping on her thighs as it comes out of her gaping ass, my glans is full of juice too.

Mother-in-law: - Show your ass Monique, mom will clean you, come Eusèbe too.

Monique gets up and presents her ass to her mother who is still sitting on the couch, Luce licks everything with application, she also sticks her tongue in the dilated hole, then it's my turn, I get my cock cleaned by my mother-in-law's tongue.

Mother-in-law: - Come on, Monique my dear, you will eat here with us, your father will be back soon, prepare something quickly.

And so ends this beautiful session. I'm dealing with two beautiful pigs, I just hope I can do it again soon.

MY PURIFICATION

I will tell you about an adventure that happened to me when I was 18 years old.

I was a shy and reserved young man with a strict upbringing, characterized above all by a lack of sexual education.

All I had seen of women was when I walked on the beach during the vacations.

I was always aroused by the pubic hair that sprouted from my bathing suit.

It just so happened that every year the parish community held a fair in which I participated by holding a booth.

That year, the parish priest had asked me to help Mrs. Germaine D, a bigot, in the general organization of this festival.

She was a woman who had been a widow for about ten years and was 65 years old.

She had a rather hard face, but what was fascinating about her was that she was very tall and very strong.

She also had a huge chest, which was borderline abnormal but that fascinated me.

So we made an appointment and I went to her house on a Wednesday in the early afternoon.

She lived in a small house in the woods.

When I arrived at her house, I noticed a car that wasn't hers; it was that of another village bigot, Marie Paule, also quite tall and with an imposing chest.

When Germaine opened the door, I was very surprised by her attire; she was in a tennis skirt with a sweater that hid her breasts; given the rocking and my glance through the recess I noticed that she was not wearing a bra; as with Marie Paule, the same tennis skirt with a shitty t-shirt through which the areolas of her breasts could be seen.

We sat in the living room; me in the armchair; them on the couch opposite me.

For about an hour we talked about the fair but I found it hard to concentrate because they were spreading their legs and I could see their crotches without panties.

I must admit I was in a state of great excitement and my tracksuit showed a significant bulge.

Around 3:30 p.m. Germaine offered me a coffee which I gladly accepted.

Her friend took the opportunity to ask me about my friends in the kitchen.

I stammered that I wasn't thinking about it and immediately asked if I was a virgin; I was completely shocked because such words in her mouth seemed unseemly; I replied that I was, despite my insistence.

Germaine returned with the coffee.

When I picked up my cup, I was so confused that I spilled the coffee on my tracksuit.

Germaine came over to me and said: "Wait, take off your tracksuit, you'll burn yourself, I'll lend you one of my son's who left it the last time he was here".

She went to get it; meanwhile, Marie Paule rushed to take it off me.

I was standing, she pushed me onto the couch and removed my pants; just as she finished, Germaine entered the room.

What I didn't anticipate was that as I pulled my underpants up my panties would also come down.

I found myself with my sex erect with the two women looking at it.

Germaine came over to me and said, "But the little guy is getting excited.

I didn't know where I was but I was in a state of incredible excitement.

Germaine gently took my sex with her hand and began to masturbate me; I felt like I was going to explode, but before I had time to say wow, she had introduced my sex into her mouth and began to pump it.

Less than 2 minutes later I started to cum, I tried to pull my cock out of her mouth but she held me down and drank every last drop.

At a later time I turned to Marie Paule who had undressed.

She said, "Come, my darling, come suck me." I approached her and began to suck her breasts violently.

She asked me to be gentle and I felt the tip harden.

She guided my hand to her sex; my finger was soon covered in secretion.

She began to moan and took my head which she placed at the level of her sex.

She then opened her lips and asked me to suck her clit.

I found the taste quite pleasant, she obviously liked it a lot and after a few minutes she came with a loud scream; I received the fruit of her pleasure on my tongue and face.

I didn't mind Germaine who, when I turned around, was also naked; she had an absolutely magnificent body for a guy like me; her breasts were huge and even though they dropped a bit, they excited me so I started to get hard again.

But what was amazing was that she had brought a small stool with an exceptional contraption on it.

It was an ebony dildo that was at least 35 cm long and had a diameter of 8 cm; she asked me to do the same thing to her as to Marie Paule. As I approached her I saw that she had coated the dildo with gel and was beginning to push it into her anus as she sat on it; She seemed to get great pleasure from it and pulled my head violently towards her sex; I held her hips and sucked her clit, I went up and down in rhythm with the introduction of the object into her anus

At one point she screamed in pleasure and released her cum on my tongue, which she asked me to swallow.

But I wasn't out of the woods yet.

She withdrew from the object on which Marie Paule impaled herself with pleasure; obviously they were used to the object.

While Marie Paule was masturbating while being fucked by the object, Germaine had put my cock between her breasts and was jerking me off.

I ended up ejaculating into a glass from which she collected the fruit of my second orgasm.

Everyone slumped down on the couch.

I was about to leave, but they didn't see it that way; I had to go home, but Germaine phoned my parents and told them we had work to do, that she was keeping me at dinner to work until 10pm; my parents had no idea that the two bigots were educating me.

Germaine carried me in her arms as if I were a baby and laid me down on her old canopy bed; she told me she would be back; looking around, I saw that there were anchor points on the bed and in a display case a collection of olisbos ranging from 10 cm to 35 cm with increasing diameters.

I was really becoming the plaything of some real sluts.

Both of them returned to the room after half an hour and woke me up by licking my sex and sucking my cock greedily

When they judged that I was of sufficient size, they got on all fours and I penetrated their vaginas in turn, I took a little longer but ended up cumming in Marie Paule's vagina.

Not being satisfied, they took the opportunity to start a somewhat surprising 69 sex position; while they titillated each other's clitoris with their tongues, they asked me to introduce my fist in turn into their anus and more and more violently

I found it shocking but they seemed to love it and eventually they both came.

Germaine got up and started talking to me in a nasty tone

You know you hurt our back, you deserve to be punished, don't you think Marie Paule?

Yes, I know," she replied.

Germaine lifted me from the bed and took me on her lap, asking me to nurse her like a baby.

In the meantime, I saw Marie Paule in a mirror installing a hammock shape in the anchor points of the bedpost.

Germain lifted me up and laid me down on it, asking me not to move; I was beginning to worry when she pinned my ankles and wrists and I found myself in the position of being ripped apart.

I then heard Germaine say, "Are we going to punish our little baby now?

First they made me drink my sperm and told me that I couldn't hold back with them and that I should do the same.

I drank my cum and also found that it tasted good.

Then they started licking my anus and said "you'll see, you'll like it".

They smeared gel on my anus and then they inserted in turn a finger, then two, then three, in my anus, which hurt but the gel they put afterwards had the gift of relieving the pain

Germaine and Marie Paule had inserted two fingers each into my anus, which when they turned them around gave me a form of pleasure

Then I saw Germaine take the dildos from the display case and the two women insert one into my already large anus.

I was in a state of mind and they were enjoying inserting larger and larger ones;

At one point, while I still had a dildo in my anus, they untied me and Marie Paule took me into the living room while continuing to handle the dildo in my anus;

Then I saw Germaine polishing the dildo that was on the small stool by coating it with gel

She came back to me, removed the device from my anus and smeared my ass and the inside of my anus with gel

Since they were very nice to me, I let myself go, they even took the opportunity to take turns performing frenzied fellatio.

At one point, as I was regaining my strength, I saw them stand up and grab me each with one leg in their hands and me with my arms on each of their shoulders

They lifted me up and I knew immediately what they were going to do.

Germaine told me 'there is no need to shout, we are in the middle of the forest'.

They gently carried me over the dildos.

I could feel the huge device at the height of my anus, they were lowering and lifting me;

I lost some consciousness as the device penetrated me.

I woke up when they started pushing inside me and pulling me up

They were reasonable and only got 8 inches into my anus.

This obviously put them in such a state of arousal that they ended up pulling me out;

They laid down on the floor and inserted my still erect sex into their vaginas, moving me from one to the other.

Just as I was about to cum, Germaine lifted me up and slid my sex into Marie Paule's mouth, in which I ended up ejaculating.

We ended up having dinner.

They asked me to never say what had happened and I had to undergo further treatment for a few more months

The next day, I had a very painful anus; I went to the doctor, who was a woman, not knowing how to explain my condition

She reassured me by saying? You know, I saw you go back to Germaine, you're not the first virgin they have denuded and I'm always there to help the poor unfortunate?

The doctor was another adventure that was nowhere near as interesting as the one I had experienced with my two bigots.

THE UNIVERSITY EXAM

That day I went to work with Nico; we were preparing for the university exams together. We were doing very, very well and it was quite difficult to actually work. We could easily talk about other things, start rambling and, as a result, we didn't get much work done.

Several times I had already wondered if there was just friendship between us or not, but we never really talked about it. I knew he had a girlfriend (I'd met her once or twice at parties) that he'd been with for a while and, from what he'd told me, it was going pretty well. So even though sometimes I felt like there should have been more between us, I didn't tell him.

I didn't know what he was thinking either. Sometimes he acted like a young man would when he was trying to seduce a young girl. And I wasn't insensitive to that...but I didn't give in to what I took to be anticipation, because it might not be.

Anyway, while we were trying to work, I couldn't help but think about throwing myself into his arms and begging him to kiss me, cuddle me, and all sorts of other things. But then I would see pictures of him with Julia, his girlfriend, all over the walls and shelves of his living room, and my mind got the better of my desires and fantasies.

We had been there about two hours (or trying to, anyway) when Julia came in. I watched Nico as she walked into the room: it was like he was seeing an apparition.

And it's true that she was beautiful: tall and very well built, with long red hair that swayed to the middle of her back, surrounding her angelic face in which her big half-gray, half-green eyes sparkled with happiness but also with mischief; she wore a thin, blue dress that revealed just enough of her beautiful body, but in which her breasts seemed to be tight. I think any guy would have fallen in love with her completely, she was so beautiful and attractive.

She walked over to us, vaguely glancing at all our school stuff on the table in front of us. Then she kissed her sweetie and said hello to me too.

I thought I'd find you alone," she said almost disappointedly to Nico, "but I actually find you in charming company, pretending to revise....

I assure you we are really working," she replied.

'We're trying, anyway...' I added.

She looked at me for a long time with his fiery eyes. Her gaze was urgent, almost accusatory. I got the impression that she was tacitly asking me if I had done 'something wrong' with her treasure. But eventually he took his eyes off me and turned them on Nico. After a few seconds, without saying a word, she walked over to him, put one leg between his, then leaned in and kissed him fiercely, almost falling on top of him. Se wallowed a little more on the couch next to me and she lay a little more on top of him, without their mouths separating.

I watched them do it, indiscreetly, but telling myself it was just one long reunion kiss that wouldn't last forever. But it was much more impressive: undoubtedly under pressure from Julia, Nico lay down almost completely on the couch, leaving only the small corner where I was sitting free, and his legs falling next to mine. Then Julia stood up, and I saw her lift her dress slightly and bring her hands along her thighs, pulling up a pair of white panties.

I couldn't believe it!

I'm not disturbing you, am I?" I asked, probably a little stupidly.

But Julia was already climbing on her boyfriend. She replied, "No, no, don't worry about it..." very naturally, as she lifted up her dress again and knelt down, facing me, with her thighs spread wide, right over Nico's face. I think I must have looked really funny. I was completely frozen, paralyzed with surprise, and stood there with my mouth open, watching Julia slowly wiggle and stiffen from time to time, no doubt under the oral assault of her sweetheart.

She was pretty much in control of herself, though, as she didn't scream and just moaned a little. And as I recovered my senses and was finally about to get up and walk out of this room, she started talking openly to me:

So, Delphine, is it? I hope I didn't interrupt you too much in your revisions?

I didn't answer, still in a state of hallucination. He continued, a little cynically:

Sometimes she would pause between words and emit a little moan, which betrayed what she was really doing. She also began to fondle her two large breasts briskly, right in front of me, kneading them firmly through her dress. I couldn't take my eyes off her; yet I had an urge to get up and get out. But she kept talking to me:

Ah, I was craving sex. Hmm, if you only knew how good it felt to feel her tongue swirling inside me.

I wanted to respond that I would love to know.... I was still struggling between my desire to leave and slam the door, and the irresistible feeling of attraction that was urging me to stay. Nico wasn't moving at all, you would have thought he was dead. His arms seemed to be trapped under his girlfriend's thighs, and his body only rose with the fairly rapid but regular rhythm of his breathing. But on closer inspection, he had a very impressive sort of lump in his groin. She had often bragged to me about the size of her sex, in a joking way, but what I saw seemed to confirm her claims.

Julia had also seen what I was looking at and had seen that I was looking at him. Stifling a few more sighs of pleasure, she managed to whisper to me:

Don't you want to see this beautiful thing?

I still didn't blink. She continued:

Unbutton her jeans and you'll get a surprise.... A big surprise, too....

I didn't know where I was anymore. It was really crazy. My eyes went from that bulge in her pants to Julia being licked right in front of me. Her dress came down to her thighs, but still hid most of it, as well as Nico's neck and head.

If you don't want to do it for yourself, do it for me. I don't want to move, I'm fine here.

The bulge on her jeans seemed to have gotten even bigger. I couldn't stand to see this girl I barely knew getting off on a guy I wanted, and whose cock was poking out right in front of me, under a pair of unfortunate jeans that were just waiting to be opened. And Julia was moaning louder and more often. She was no longer holding back from fully expressing her pleasure.

Hmmm... Come on, aaahhh... Pull out his cock, oooohh... yes... let's enjoy it... aaahh... don't tell me you don't want it....

It was all too much for me. I had no idea where I was or what I was doing. I only had one idea left in my head: to pull this thing that was swelling Nico's ass out of its hole. I almost jumped on top of him, threw both hands at the task: unbuttoning his jeans. But in my haste, I couldn't do it. I was panicking, I was getting angry, I was getting aroused.... I almost ripped the belt, then pulled with all my strength on each side of the pants so that the buttons popped off one by one.

Slowly, eagerly...

No, now that I had started, I wasn't going to stop. The pants opened and the bulge came to distort a white underwear, bigger than ever. This wasn't going to slow me down for long.... The curd had a button that allowed an opening. I literally ripped it off. And there it was, the thing was finally revealed to me: thick and long, almost all rigid. Thicker and longer than anything I'd ever seen. Thicker and longer than anything I had ever imagined. And almost fully stretched, it was still hardening in my hands, I could feel it still swelling.

Julia was still talking to me, but I wasn't listening at all. I was carefully masturbating that magnificent cock and already imagining myself enjoying it to the fullest. I like it a lot. But Julia probably wouldn't have wanted to at this moment.... Julia... How lucky she was to have all this for herself.... Besides, it was too much for her alone.... She shouldn't have kept it to herself....

I couldn't control my thoughts. Julia... I recovered for a moment and looked fearfully towards her. She seemed to be at the height of her pleasure. She looked at me with eyes that seemed rather benign. I continued to masturbate her boyfriend, staring at her.

So, do you like his cock?

I nodded softly, vaguely, as if in submission.

Well, go ahead and masturbate and suck it! I want him to be completely stiff, all hard and taut.

I agreed, without thinking. I knelt down next to Nico's prone body and started pumping the huge thing as best I could. I wanted it badly, I was at my most aroused. I opened my mouth like I'd never opened it before to let the big glans rush down my throat and began a long series of strokes back and forth. Then I heard more moans, more pronounced, more masculine, mingling with Julia's still panting ones.

The cock was soon monstrously hard and swollen in my mouth. My tongue and lips slid slowly, caressing the glans and shaft. And with one hand I jerked the part I couldn't suck. I felt myself getting wetter and wetter as I pumped him faster and deeper. I could feel the desire flowing from my sex and wetting my panties. I couldn't stop pumping and jerking and the moans became louder, encouraging me to do more and more.

When I looked up, Julia was completely naked and had left her perch. Her breasts, which I had already guessed were large through the walls of her dress, were like two huge apples, heavy and swollen, and a light rusty fleece adorned her lower belly. She was standing next to the couch, looking at me with a smile. I stepped back, leaving her with her lovely sex. She walked over to me and gave me a long smooch. I let her do it.

I was no longer in control. I was crazy with excitement and desire. Then she started unbuttoning my blouse, slowly but surely, continuing to watch me. I continued to let her do it to me. I could see Nico, next to us, vaguely straightening up to try to undress.

When she took off my top, she attacked my jeans and soon I was in my panties and bra. I was very hot, I think I blushed. Then she leaned over me to reach the hooks of my bra. I had her breasts right in front of my nose and they were also pressing against my face as she unhooked the lace. I felt really weird, ashamed for sure, but at the same time I gave myself completely to her, and I was almost happy.

Once my breasts were free, she proceeded to untie my last piece of fabric and soon I was in her own dress. She kissed me again and caressed my breasts for a moment. I had always thought I had large breasts myself, but next to his they were nothing. They were nice, big, but not droopy. He kissed me again, then told me to go give his sweetie a sip of my pleasure.

He was back in his original position, lying on the couch. I moved closer to his face. I watched him discover my body for a moment: his eyes wandered over my breasts, my belly, my hips, my thighs, then my legs, and then down to my breasts.

Julia knelt on the couch, where I had been a few minutes earlier, and took her boyfriend's big cock in her hand. She started pumping it, regularly giving me a few mischievous and provocative looks.

Nico motioned me to come over to the seat he had occupied just moments before. He was offering to come and give her my sex. I too wanted to finally be taken care of. To finally feel the pleasure in me, not just the desire. I sat on her face, one knee on each side of her head, facing Julia who was still sucking him off. Almost immediately I felt her tongue gently slide over the entrance to my sex, before moving more completely inside me. I let out all my happiness.

I moaned, rubbing my breasts and watching Julia as she lavished her favors on the huge thing. Apparently she was doing it wonderfully well, because I could feel Nico squeaking between my thighs, and her body suddenly jerked upward from time to time, as if in a spasm.

But soon she stopped (I had no real sense of time, but I don't think much time had passed), straightened up, and came to impale herself right in front of me on the still monstrously swollen cock. She must have been really wet because she sank into it in one go, probably to the depths of her body, making her howl with pleasure. Then she gave her pelvis a slow, steady up and down motion and sighed in ecstasy, just as Nico moaned underneath me every time her beautiful body descended around his.

Unperturbed, however, he continued to lick my pussy. And I continued to cum under the effects of his oral caresses. Julia came to me and kissed me. We made love long and hard on top of our lover who was making us both cum. And as she kissed me, she caressed my breasts. I did the same and put my hands on her huge breasts, which I kneaded for a moment, then caressed more gently.

But suddenly she stood up and abandoned her position (which seemed so pleasant to me). The big cock fell brutally onto its owner's belly. I let myself lick it for a few more moments, watching Julia who had started pumping the thing again. However, she soon abandoned it and came to me. She kissed me again; her kiss tasted like her own.

Then, under her guidance, I straightened up and knelt down again, but this time facing the back of the couch, leaning against its backrest. Nico had stood up and I was now presenting my rear to him, my thighs still wide open. Then I felt two fingers enter me deeply. I moaned a little as they circled in my sex.

I went to turn around to see who they belonged to, but they immediately withdrew from my body, and I felt something much larger rubbing against my slit. At the same time, Julia came around the couch and stood in front of me. Nico's cock was now pressing harder against my slit. He was starting to push inside me, slowly. My lips opened like never before to make room for the huge glans. Then the rest of his sex invaded my vagina, slowly, until it was completely filled.

I had screamed as he entered me, my eyes fixed on Julia's, standing in front of me. I had her breasts right under my nose. She was looking at me too; I could see in her eyes that she was enjoying seeing me feel so much pleasure. Then Nico started literally pounding my pussy, at full speed. His cock was as hard and tense as ever and he came three times a second deep into my sex. I hadn't stopped moaning since he had entered me. It felt wonderfully good. I was giving myself completely to him and his cock.

This went on for a good five minutes, during which he fucked me at full speed. And Julia pressed her breasts to my face and urged me to lick them, suck them, kiss them. And when I wasn't devouring her tits, she was giving me her fingers to suck on, as if they had been a cock she had stuck in her pussy before presenting them to me.

Either way, I was at the height of happiness. Her cock felt so good. I had never had so much good given to me at one time. But when he suddenly withdrew from my body, I was exhausted. He released me and I collapsed on my back on the couch, as if I had died. It was as if I was in a dream, my eyes fixed on the ceiling, watching without seeing.

Julia's face suddenly appeared upside down in front of my eyes. She leaned over me and kissed me again, and again I knew from the taste of her kiss that she had probably just sucked her boyfriend once more. Then her face dropped in front of my eyes, and her hair came to caress my forehead, then my cheeks, and then I felt her heavy breasts come to touch the top of my head.

One of them slid down my face, then stopped and crashed right into my mouth. I started to devour it, just as Julia pounced on mine, devouring those as well.

I also felt my thighs being gently spread. I was still letting go. Then her hands slid between my legs. A few fingers occasionally ventured inside me, then came out and spread all my happiness along my parting. Then I felt something infinitely softer come to my sex. Squeezing my thighs together, I imagined Nico giving me the full oral experience.

After a while, Julia stood up a little. Her breasts escaped my grasp and I saw them continue to descend in front of my face. Soon her hair was running down my belly, lower and lower, and her breasts were hitting mine. Then I had her belly in front of my eyes. And then I felt one knee take its place gently next to my head and then another. Her hair reached my lower belly as the fleece of her sex covered my eyes. He continued to move slowly, inexorably. I wanted to move, but I didn't have the strength. She moved forward a few more inches and I had her parting before my eyes. I felt her dip her head between my thighs. A few more inches. And her lips latched onto the lips of my sex. Her tongue began to thrust into my belly, swirling and lapping rapidly.

I immediately had an immense feeling of intense pleasure. I closed my eyes to better savor this new pleasure. The smell of his sex was wafting around me. A powerful and strong smell. I moaned softly under the caresses he was offering me. I tightened my thighs around her head, my way of telling her I wanted more.

She probably wanted me to lick her too, but I didn't want that at all. But when I opened my eyes again, after a few seconds, I saw Nico's huge cock swinging between Julia's sex and my mouth. His glans moved closer to me and bounced a few times against my cheeks or chin. Tipping my head back, I opened my mouth wide and welcomed him deep into my throat where he went back and forth a few times, making his owner moan for a long time.

But he pulled out fast enough to dive into Julia's-soaked pussy, which was still licking mine. We all started moaning and groaning louder and louder. Nico's sex was sinking in and out of his girlfriend faster and faster. I now had his balls, also oversized and all swollen, going back and forth in front of my nose and eyes. And regularly pulling out of her sweetheart's body to offer me to suck on his glans that was always incredibly swollen, and soaked in the pleasure and happiness she was letting flow from her.

Soon, guided again by Julia, I let myself roll onto my side and Nico abandoned my mouth and her pussy. We found ourselves in the opposite position: she was lying on her back, and I was lying on top of her. She was still licking me and I started pumping Nico's pussy again for a few seconds. But eventually he pulled away, apparently intending to surround our two intertwined bodies.

I was now alone with Julia's side, which was still licking me. I started stroking her with one hand, running my fingers from her clit to the entrance of her ass, and pushed a couple of fingers into her slit, then started rubbing her clit again. Soon I felt my hips being gripped; Julia stopped licking me and the huge cock entered me again, more gently than before, but just as intensely. Julia went back to licking what she could, the top of my slit and my clit.

I was cumming even more than I had a few minutes before. And I was moaning at least as much. I also kept rubbing a hand between my partner's legs. I was again at the height of pleasure, excitement and happiness. And sometimes I would lick the fingers I placed on her.

Suddenly, without understanding what I was doing, I plunged my head completely between her thighs. I wanted to taste what that intoxicating smell gave off. And when my tongue sank between Julia's lips, I heard her moan in turn. I licked her sex once and then again. My happiness continued to grow as Nico's cock strokes became more and more violent, fast and deep. I slid my tongue into that hot sex again, which was blissful in front of me.

Julia had tightened her thighs around my head, telling me to keep licking her. Which I did. And I liked it. It was like an extra dose of arousal and made my pleasure even better.

But suddenly it stopped. Nico withdrew from me completely. I waited a while, thinking Julia was sucking him again, and continued licking. And I heard Nico moan; it seemed to confirm that Julia was taking care of him. I felt the fingers enter my vagina again. They danced there for a while and then came out and spread my wetness all along my parting. Then the fingers went back into my sex and came out again, this time forcing their way directly into my anus. But they were so wet that they went in without a problem. I arched my back a little as they entered me from there, not expecting it.

Soon they were out and I felt the huge cock sliding along my wall as well. He probably wanted to sodomize me, but I really didn't want to. The thing was too big and it was going to hurt too much. Julia held my ass firmly and I could feel more fingers jerking my pussy and ass again. This went on for a long time, during which I was still tasting my partner's sex. Julia started licking me again, but I had no idea where Nico had gone. I soon had the answer, because while I was busy licking my girlfriend's hot sex, I saw his cock coming towards me, more swollen than ever.

I immediately dropped what I was doing and rushed to suck that thing again. I wanted more. I wanted more. I pumped it again. And Nico was masturbating at the same time. The cock was going in and out of my mouth, rubbing against my teeth and coming against the back of my throat, then coming out almost completely, and then going back in even faster, even deeper. And Julia continued to pleasure me on the other side.

It all happened very quickly. I felt Nico twitch and his cock stiffen. And with a scream louder than I had ever heard, I felt him release. A liberating explosion. A few hot, powerful spurts, deep into my mouth. And then a few more slightly less dense spurts that landed on my face and Julia's thighs and buttocks. She had sensed that this was the climax; she was pushing more fingers into my ass and pussy than ever before. And I was squealing under the onslaught coming from all sides.

I swallowed what was left in my mouth, then got up and went to kiss Julia. I wanted her to know that I had taken it all and I wanted her to lick what was left of my face. And we kissed, licked, and caressed each other for a long time before we fell into a deep, dreamless sleep.

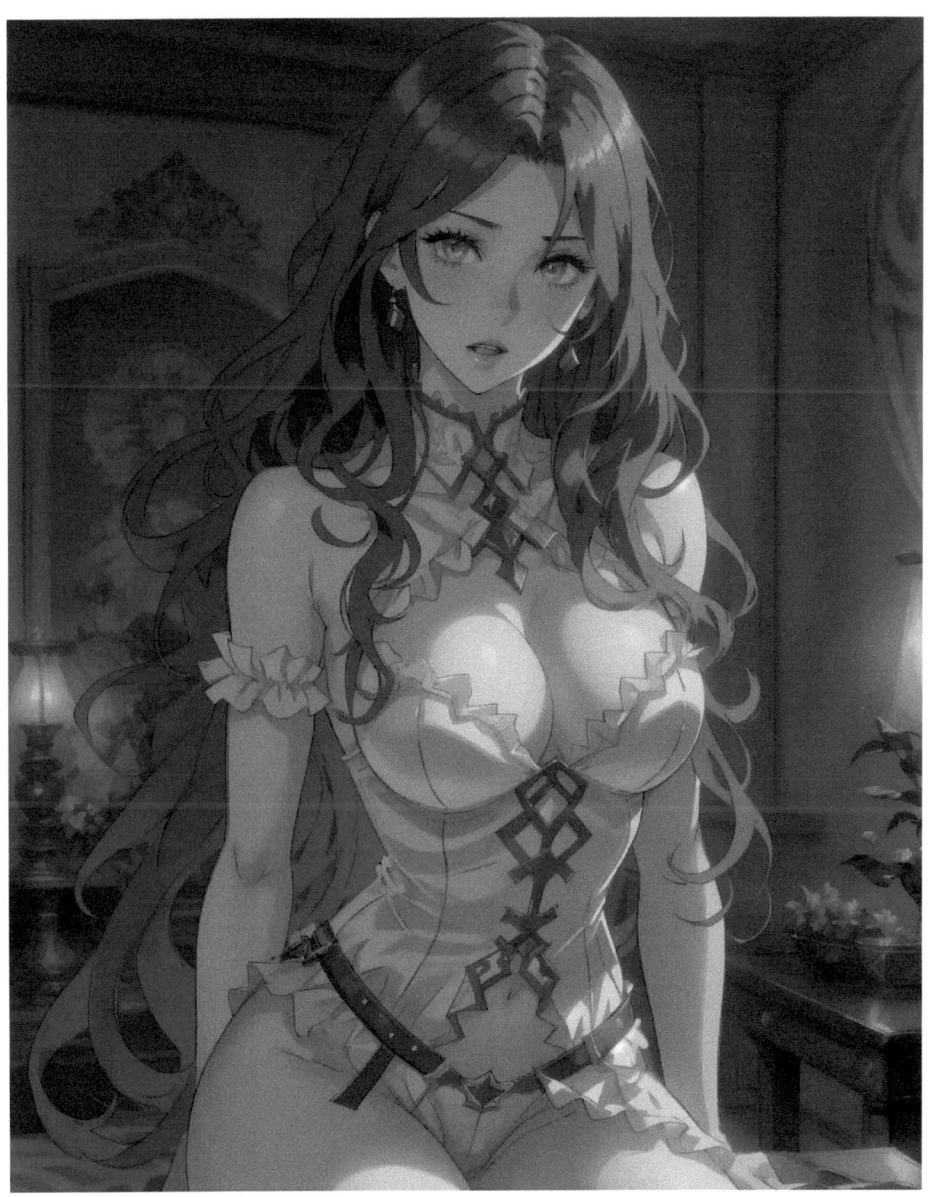

TWO BEAUTIFUL WOMEN FOR HIM

Last week I had invited Aurélie, my best friend, to spend the evening at home to distract herself after a few days of hard work at the dealership.

We had spent the evening discussing our respective stories when we got to talking about David, a mutual friend. It happened that a few days later he was hosting a dinner party at his house, to which we were invited to celebrate his graduation. In fact, he had been an Italian teacher for several years and was preparing for this exam in parallel so that he could teach at a university as he had always wanted to do.

David was a very handsome man, typically Italian, about thirty years old. He had dark hair, big black eyes, dark skin, a well-muscled body and above all a little Italian accent that made me literally fall in love with him when I talked to him.

Aurelie confessed to me during our conversation that she also had a great attraction to our friend and that she dreamed of having an adventure with him. Then I suggested a little game that would really entertain our friend David and both of us at the same time. He was very excited about the idea and went home.

A few days later, we met again at David's house. We were a good ten guests at this meal. David welcomed us divinely, with beautiful decorations, succulent food, and quality wines. Once the dinner was over, the other guests disappeared one by one until only Aurélie, David and I were left.

Having one last drink in the lounge, we told him that we had a little surprise for him. Very intrigued and interested, he then told us that he was ready to receive this mysterious surprise without further ado.

Giving Aurelie a small smile, I moved closer to her and kissed her passionately. Completely astonished, David stared at us, not quite knowing how to react, but he still remained attentive to the show we were offering him.

Aurelie was very beautiful. She had long curly black hair, beautiful blue eyes and a body that would make any man fantasize. That night she wore a long navy blue dress, split with beautiful thin heels and very sexy lingerie for all of us. As for me, I had my blonde hair tied back and wore a short black dress that showed off my breasts and long legs. As for my lingerie, it was ultra sexy: garter belt, lace thong and matching bra. I felt very attractive.

Aurelie and I were still embraced as she caressed me by sliding my beautiful dress down to my ankles. She ran her hands over my chest and I could feel my breasts protruding from the growing desire inside me. She was kneading my breasts as she caressed my neck with her tongue and stopped with the tips of her nails on my hardened nipples. All the while I was caressing her buttocks and breasts over her dress, until I removed it to reveal her beautifully sculpted body.

Then I continued my hand games as I slipped on her thong, making sure David could see what we were doing. We were getting really hot and it got worse when he reached down my thong to stroke my pussy.

She rolled my clit between two fingers like an expert and pushed one into my wet vagina in places as she moaned a little. I in turn began stroking her hot pussy and digging into her crotch as I circled her hard clit to give her indescribable pleasure in front of our friend.

David was really getting hard. I could see that his cock was hard through his pants and as I touched Aurelie's burning pussy and she penetrated me with her fingers, I was thinking about the moment when that big cock would sink into my hole and then into Aurelie's.

Very excited by this hard scene, David approached us. We were still stroking our hot pussies, spreading our big lips so that he could see the details of our completely wet pussies. We then started undressing him until he was completely naked in front of both of our hot bodies. We sat him down on the couch and stroked him. Aurelie touched his superbly muscular torso as she licked him, while I felt his hard cock in a steady back and forth motion with one hand and with the other held his balls and gently kneaded them.

Then Aurelie reached for his cock and put it in her mouth and sucked it while she jerked him off. Slowly at first, then faster and faster. I, meanwhile, was stroking Aurelie and moving to her still-soaked pussy. I began licking her as I pushed three fingers into her desire-dilated vagina. I licked her clit with my tongue and then sucked it a little hard, spreading saliva all over her sex to make her cum.

Aurelie continued her wonderful fellatio and I moved closer to David's cock to suck it too, then she started licking his balls while I sucked him in turn.

Her body swayed with pleasure to better accompany the movements of our mouths against his hot, hard cock. The three of us were burning with desire for each other, my Aurelie was licking my pussy while I sucked David.

She was devouring me all over, literally eating my pussy by sucking my clit and then sliding his whole tongue and fingers into my vagina flooded with pleasure.

After these games of saliva, David took Aurelie from behind. He pushed his cock deep into her wet ass. Screaming like crazy, David accelerated his penetrations and fucked Aurelie with his huge cock. The pleasure was immense, all three of us were wet with saliva and excitement and the penetrations were fast, deep and increasingly pleasurable. We were wild and all three of us were moaning with pleasure. Aurelie was spread wide open and had her ass bitten until we both reached orgasm. David ejaculated into Aurelie's burning ass with a cry of pleasure.

Exhausted from our incendiary play, we collapsed on the couch to get some rest before heading home, obviously promising to do it again very soon. Mmmmmm can't wait for the next time!